The Earl in Winter

By Kathryn Le Veque

Part One of The Brother

KATHRYN LE VEQUE
NOVELS

ARE YOU SIGNED UP FOR KATHRYN'S BLOG?

You'll get the latest news and information on exclusive giveaways, exclusive excerpts, coming releases, sales, free books, cover reveals and more.

Kathryn's blog followers get it all first. No spam, no junk.

Get the latest info from the reigning Queen of English Medieval Romance.

Sign Up Here
kathrynleveque.com

FOREWORD

If you've read *Outlander*, then you know something of the Jacobite uprising, but if not, suffice it to say that it's a turbulent time in England/Scotland history. The Battle of Culloden Moor was the last civil war battle fought upon UK soil.

The battle itself was a horrific rout. About 6,000 Jacobites comprised of Highlanders, French, and even English troops faced about 6,000 British troops on a cold spring morning upon the Culloden moor on April 16, 1746. In a nutshell, the Jacobites started first with sporadic cannon fire, which provoked a nasty response from the British. They fired off what were known as canister shot, which were essentially canisters filled with musket balls, turning the cannons into a massive shotgun. Canister shot mowed down entire groups of Jacobites, but it was the High-landers who got the worst of it. They were fearless as few men are, but they were no match for the superior British forces.

There were piles of dead on the fields of Culloden, Highlanders who were buried where they fell, with the local church doing what they could for the rest of the wounded, English included. The Highlander casualties were somewhere around 1,500 to 2,000, while the British casualties were significantly less – only 50 reported dead. In the days following the battle, the British spared no expense in hunting down Jacobite rebels because, at that point, the wars were over and the Jacobite cause was dead.

Now, imagine the first holiday season after Culloden, that horrible battle that took so many lives. Imagine those in a small village on the road leading to the battlefield, trying to find the holiday spirit in such a year. In fact, a law was passed in 1640 making Yuletide illegal, so surely that only made the season more difficult.

In this collection, we'll peek into the world of the only tavern in the village of Calvine, a place called Balthazar's Inn. The inhabitants are still reeling, as are the visitors, in more ways than one can imagine. There are secrets here, some left untold, some better off exposed, but the spirit of holidays is still there amongst the turmoil. No battle, and no laws, can suppress the goodness, peace, and joy that is the very essence of the holiday season.

It is a time of change in the Highlands of Scotland.

Welcome to A Very Highland Holiday.

The Earl in Winter

When James de Lohr heads into the wilds of Scotland to discover what happened to his brother at the Battle of Culloden, his stay at Balthazar's Tavern has an unexpected twist. On a night when angels walk the earth, James comes face to face with his very own guardian angel.

AUTHOR'S NOTE

The Earl in Winter is about a descendant of my big Medieval family, the House of de Lohr (de Lohr Dynasty). It's one of my oldest houses, and most popular, and I love the fact that I was able to bring this family forward a few hundred years. They're alpha-male, sword-toting, fun-loving, battle-driven knights (at least, in Medieval times, they are), and it's been really cool to see that the tradition of military service with the family hasn't wavered.

What's even cooler is the fact that the fabulous Kerrigan Byrne has written the companion story to this tale in this very collection – The Earl of Christmas Past. While my tale is about the younger brother, James, Kerrigan's tale is about the older brother, Johnathan. Two brothers, two tales, two earls, and worlds apart (literally).

I hope you enjoy this poignant, tender, and sometimes tearful tale of love – of brotherly love, and also the love between a hero and his heroine.

Happy Reading!

Part One

BALTHAZAR'S INN

December 17, 1746
Calvine, Scotland

A LL HE'D DONE was open the entry door.
That was apparently enough of an invitation for someone to throw a stool at his head.

James de Lohr ducked swiftly, stumbling back out of the door and narrowly avoiding being hit by a man who came hurtling through the opening after him.

But it wasn't an attack – it was because the man had been struck in what was surely a tavern fight to end all tavern fights. He was simply flying with the momentum. James jumped out of the way as another man came flying through the door right after him.

And somewhere in the middle of the chaos, James heard a scream.

There was a woman inside Balthazar's Inn, trapped in the midst of a nasty fight. It was just past sunset on what should have been a peaceful snowy winter's eve and the fists were flying in the low-ceilinged, stuffy common room. All James could see were figures moving about, punching and kicking and grunting. As he stood at the open door, part of a table came flying at him and he deftly knocked it down.

Hell of a party, he thought wryly.

Another scream caught his attention.

This time, the noise was off to his left and, instinctively, he moved towards the sound of distress. He was a military man, an officer, and a very good one. If there was trouble, he was sworn to assist.

Even in the middle of a bar fight.

And then, he saw it.

A woman with frizzy red hair hiding behind a small table as a man grabbed at her. She was using the table like a shield, shoving it at him, forcing him to keep his distance. James grabbed the man by the hair, yanking him away from the woman. As the man stumbled back, James could see that there was a second woman cowering behind the table also.

"C-Come with me," he said over the noise.

The woman balked. "Away with ye or I'll knock the senses from ye!"

James avoided a flying piece of wood. "L-Lady, I assure you, it is only to take you to safety. O-Or do you want to stay in this midst of this tempest?"

The woman paused for an indecisive moment until a candlestick hurled through the air, hitting the wall behind her. That seemed to make her decision for her. With a reluctant nod, she came out from behind the table, pulling her companion with her.

Using his big body as a human shield, James herded the women out of the tavern. It was freezing outside, however, as the snow began to fall more heavily than before. More furniture met its demise as it slammed against the door frame and the women shrieked as wood splintered.

"I-I fear if we remain, we will be subject to more violence," James said. "W-We must find a place of safety."

The woman with the red hair grabbed the woman next to her, beckoning to him. "This way!"

James followed.

Through the slush and snow, they went around to the rear of the tavern. At one point, James slipped in the abundant mud, steadying himself against the stone structure. The tavern itself was unremarkable, squat and thick-walled, with a steeply pitched roof. With snowflakes falling in his eyes, he managed to follow the women through the rear entrance.

They ended up in the kitchen. The heat was like a slap in the face, in sharp contrast to the cold outside. James cleared his eyes, noting the big chamber and roaring hearth. It smelled like roasting meat. As he noted that the door leading into the common room had been shut and bolted, undoubtedly to keep out the insurrecting patrons, the woman with the red hair waved an arm at him.

"Come," she said. "This way."

Again, he followed. In hindsight, it wasn't the brightest thing to do, but he was cold and had come a very long way, and the last thing he wanted to do was stand out in the snow while the common room of the only tavern in town was torn apart.

Therefore, he followed the women into a sculler, and then into a connecting chamber. That chamber had a table, a couple of chairs, and a hearth that was burning low, but it was giving off enough heat to stave off the chill.

James stood in the doorway, looking around.

"W-What is this place?" he asked.

The redhead dropped to her knees in front of the fire and began to stoke it. "This is where my da and I eat," she said. "Sometimes the servants, too. It's not much, but it's warm and dry and away from the madness."

She was referring to the common room. James had two heavy saddlebags slung over his shoulder and he put them on the table.

"W-What happened out there?" he asked. "What started the battle?"

The redhead looked at him, her gaze lingering on him as if to get a good look at him. Tall, blond, and well-built, he was a vastly handsome specimen. "Ye're not from here," she finally said.

"N-Nay."

"Where are ye from, English?"

"Herefordshire."

"Ye're a long way from home."

"I-I am."

Without being invited to, he removed his heavy cloak, revealing another woolen coat beneath that. His gloves came off, as did his tricorne hat. He pulled off the woolen coat, too, hanging it on a peg along with the cloak to dry out. Left in a linen shirt and undershirt, breeches and boots, he sat down near the fire because he was chilled to the bone.

All the while, the redhead was watching him with the expression of a hunter sighting prey. They didn't often see such fine looking men this far north, so the young lord's appearance was a treat for the eyes. She was inherently curious.

Perhaps even a little interested.

"What's yer name, m'laird?" she asked.

He ran a hand through his damp hair. "D-De Lohr," he said. "J-James de Lohr."

"I'm Carrie," she said. "My da owns this place. He's the Balthazar on the sign. Are ye traveling through?"

He shook his head. "N-Nay," he said. "I-I've reached my destination. What was that fight about in the common room?"

He was shifting the subject, unwilling to speak further about himself. Carrie returned to the fire, but she would look for another opportunity to probe him.

"Who knows?" she said. "Someone says a wrong word and the fists fly. Only yesterday, the common room was torn up by a terrible tempest. It even tore up some of the other chambers, too."

James caught movement out of the corners of his eyes, turning to see the second woman in the room as she moved towards the hearth to help Carrie. She had been sitting in the shadows, perhaps stunned from their flight from the common room, and had only now regained her breath. Whatever the case, she was now on her feet.

He took a second look at this lass.

With brown hair, brown eyes, and lush lips, she was worth the second look. She wore a faded skirt that might have been a shade of green at one time, a leather girdle, and a linen blouse. She was also wearing a tattered woolen shawl, something with armholes in it so she could keep it on as she worked and not have it fall away. She was clearly poor in dress, but clean and most decidedly pretty.

Something about her had his attention.

"H-How long have you lived here, Carrie?" he asked, his gaze still on the other woman.

Carrie waved the other woman away as she tried to help, sending her for food and drink. As she left the chamber, Carrie replied.

"All my life," she said. "This tavern has been in my family since the days of my grandfather."

"T-Then you were here when the battle happened."

Her movements slowed. "What battle?"

"Culloden."

"I was here."

"Y-You must have seen the armies coming through town," he said. "B-British as well as the rebels. This road leads directly to the battlefield."

She turned to look at him. "Y-Ye're a long way from home, m'laird," she said. "In this village, we dunna refer tae our men as rebels. Ye'd do well tae remember that."

He nodded. "P-Point taken," he said. "I-I ask for a reason, however. I will gladly pay you for information."

"What *kind* of information?"

"I-I'm looking for my brother."

Carrie stood up from the fire, brushing off her hands. "Who was yer brother?"

"H-He fought at Culloden," he said, running his hand through his hair again as he sat forward, arms resting on his knees. "H-He was killed in battle and I've come to bring him home. As I said, I'll gladly pay for any information you can provide."

Carrie's gaze lingered on him for a moment. "I see," she said quietly. "I'm sorry for ye, then. 'Twas a terrible day, it was. So many were lost."

"W-What can you tell me?" he asked, ignoring the sympathy in her tone because he didn't want a reminder about the grief he carried around like an anchor. "A-About the English dead, I mean. Do you know what happened to them?"

Her features took on a distant look but she was saved from replying when the woman with the brown eyes entered the chamber, a tray laden with food and drink in her hands. Carrie rushed to help her unburden the tray, setting everything down on the table in front of James. There was bread, butter, boiled pork, stewed turnips, and hard boiled eggs. The drink was a generous amount of ale that had a bitter taste to it.

James hardly cared. He was famished. He, too, forgot about his question as he downed half the ale before plowing into the pork. He was vaguely aware when Carrie and the other lass left him because, at the moment, it was all about stuffing his face and resting his spirit.

He'd finally made it to this horrible place.

He was going to need his strength for what was to come.

Part Two

JAMES

THREE BIG TANKARDS of the cheap ale later, and James was having trouble sitting upright.

He wasn't a big ale drinker, but he'd been forced by necessity to become one when he traveled deep into the Scottish Highlands. That was their favored drink of choice and he'd sampled a wide variety.

He sat in the little chamber in the tavern, watching the fire pop and thinking that he needed to ask for a bed but he was afraid to get up, afraid he would fall right over on his face. As he sat there, he thought he might simply lay his head on the table. It seemed as good an opportunity as any to get some much-needed rest. As he was contemplating that very thing, the chamber door opened.

Instead of Carrie or the other woman who had been serving him, a tall man in an unbleached woolen cloak entered. James didn't pay much attention to him other than to watch him for weapons. Considering the fight he'd just seen in the common room, he wasn't taking any chances. The man had a scarf around his head, which he unwound to reveal a smiling, oddly smooth face.

"May I join you?" he asked.

It was a British accent, so James figured he couldn't be too much of a threat. He nodded, motioning to the other chair. The man pulled off his cloak, his scarf, and hung both upon a peg near the hearth. Pale and slender, he sat in the chair James had indicated.

"'Tis a difficult night for man and beast," he said, holding out his hands to the fire to warm them. "I saw the common room. You are wise to be in this small chamber, away from that chaos."

James tried to nod, but it threw him off balance. "I-I walked into the chaos when I arrived."

The stranger grinned. "It looks as if the entire room has been upended."

"T-The ruffians were on the loose."

11

The stranger noted the remains of the meal before looking to James. "My name is Rafe," he said. "And you are far from home, my lord."

James glanced at him. "H-How would you know that?"

Rafe's smile broadened. "You don't speak like a Scotsman," he said. "Where are you from?"

James sighed heavily. "A-A million miles away."

"English?"

"Aye."

"You are *very* far from home," Rafe said. "Are you simply traveling to see the glories of Scotland in winter?"

James shook his head and nearly teetered off his chair. "N-Nay," he said, grabbing the table to steady himself. "I-I've come looking for someone."

"It must be important."

"I-It is."

"Can I possibly help?"

James was drunk. That was established. Unfortunately, drink had a tendency to loosen his tongue and he didn't stop to think that the man was asking a lot of questions, questions he was quite happily and freely answering. He was speaking to the man as if he had known him, and trusted him, all his life.

"N-Not unless you can bring back the dead," he said quietly.

"I see," Rafe said. "Then I am sorry for you. May I ask who has died so that I might say a prayer?"

The chamber door creaked open and the brown-haired lass appeared, again bringing more food and drink. James assumed it was for Rafe. As she sat it on the table, James leaned back in his chair and nearly fell over. Frustrated, he grabbed at the table again to steady himself.

"I-I have come to find my brother," he said. "B-Before you ask, he perished on the Culloden moor back in April of this year and my mother has not stopped weeping. I promised the woman I would find him and bring him home, and that is what I intend to do. His name is Johnathan should you care to name him in your prayers, but it will not do any good. He was not a pious man."

As the brown-eyed woman began to slowly clean up the remnants of James' meal, listening to the conversation, Rafe was focused on his inebriated tablemate.

"I am very sorry for you," he said with soft sincerity. "It is a sad mission that you are on, then. I'm sure your mother appreciates that you are a good son."

James sighed faintly, chewing on his lip because it was a bad habit of his. When he was frustrated or weary, or both, he tended to chew. His gaze was on the fire but his mind was on the brother he'd lost.

So long ago...

"A-A good son," he muttered. Then, he snorted bitterly. "I-If you must know, I am a terrible son. I was supposed to go with him, you know. My brother, I mean. To Culloden."

"Why didn't you?"

His expression was filled with regret, with irony. "I-I had been struck down by a fever," he said. "I-I could not leave my bed, so he left without me. Like a weakling, I stayed at home while he went north with the Lancaster Foot Regiment. A friend of his returned during the summer to tell us that he had been lost. And do you know *how* it happened? My heroic, foolish brother stepped in to help a failing regiment. They had lost their officers, so he went to help them. It cost him his life, the idiot. And he left me with a burden that is impossible to bear."

Rafe was listening with sorrow. "I am certain he did not do it purposely, whatever it is."

James smacked the table, pointing a finger at him. "T-That is where you are wrong," he said. "H-He never wanted the duties that were expected of him, the burdens that the title would bring him. Did I mention that? He was the Earl of Worcester and hated the trappings. And that's why he hated me."

Rafe frowned. "Hated you? I do not believe

one brother would hate another so."

James drunkenly waved him off. "T-That is where you would be wrong again," he said. "H-He hated me because I had freedom he did not. He hated me because I would never know the weight of what he had inherited. But I *do* know because those burdens are now mine. I believe he charged into that battle a-purpose simply to push those burdens onto me."

Rafe had gotten more than he bargained for when he'd asked to share a young lord's table. As he looked at the man, his expression was almost... gentle.

"What is your name?" he asked quietly.

James sighed heavily after his tirade and turned back to the fire. "J-James de Lohr, Earl of Worcester, Viscount Leominster, Warden of the South Marches, Lord Pembridge and Marston," he muttered. "A-As you have noticed, I have a catch in my speech that is unworthy of such a position, as it has been suggested to me. School masters tried to beat it out of me, but it didn't work. When Johnathan and I were young, he would tell me that I sounded like a Billy goat, which would only make it worse and when we would argue, which was frequent, I had to write him notes and letters because he would have me so flustered that I could not speak at all."

Rafe dipped his head in a sign of respect. "My

lord," he said. "It is an honor to meet you. As for your brother… sometimes, brothers fight, but the fact that you are here to find his body and bring him home proves that you love him. As I said, you are a good son. And a good brother."

James averted his gaze. "I-I have come because my mother asked it of me," he said. "T-There is no other reason. Even if I cannot find Johnathan's body, I must search for something he had on his person when he came here. Something valuable to my family."

Rafe regarded him for a moment. "If he had something valuable on his person, more than likely, it was stripped of him," he said quietly. "You are a soldier and you know this to be true. Bodies in battle are stripped."

For the first time, James showed a measure of pain in his expression, but he didn't answer. He knew that very unpleasant fact, even if he couldn't speak of it openly. To speak of it would make it real, and as much as he shared a dysfunctional relationship with his brother, he couldn't stand the thought of the man being unceremoniously stripped of his possessions, his dignity…

Everything.

"I-I know," he said, closing his eyes for a brief moment as if to ward off the mere thought. "M-My hope is that Johnathan was removed from the field of battle before the scavengers came. Perhaps there is a chance that the family heirloom is still on his body, though I know there is a good chance it is not."

"What are you looking for?"

"A-A ring."

Rafe lifted his eyebrows as if expecting more of an answer. "Just a ring?" he said. "A signet?"

But James shook his head. "N-Not *any* ring," he said. "A-A family heirloom, passed down from earl to earl. A ring with the head of a lion that has been etched into the purest gold, with rubies set into the ocular cavities as if the blood spilled by the apex predator reflected in its very eyes. At least, that is how the ring is always described, even in old family documents. The lion's head of the House of de Lohr is our mark of excellence. It is a privilege to wear it and, as the earl, it is my right. That is what I am looking for."

Rafe nodded faintly. "Then I wish you well, my lord," he said. "But what if you do not find it?"

James averted his gaze, agonizing over that very possibility. But something moved in the shadows and he looked over, realizing the serving wench with the pretty brown eyes had been in the chamber the entire time. She had cleaned up the meal, but she had never left.

She had heard everything.

Not that he cared. He'd never see her again after this night.

"Y-You, there," he said, avoiding Rafe's question. "I-I need a chamber. I will pay handsomely for the privilege."

The woman came into the light, her big eyes looking at him rather fearfully. "I will speak with Carrie, m'laird," she said. "I think that all the beds are taken, but I shall ask."

James' half-lidded gaze looked her over, the pretty brown-eyed woman who had caught his eye before. "I-I took you from the common room when there was fighting," he said. "Y-You've been like a wraith, moving in and out of this chamber. What is your name?"

"Gaira, m'laird."

"G-Gaira, if you will bring me some blankets, I can sleep right here on this floor."

The woman dashed from the chamber and James turned to Rafe, reaching out to take the last of the man's ale. In fact, Rafe hadn't touched any of the food brought, so James shoved a piece of bread into his mouth.

"W-We shall sleep this night," he said, chewing the bread. "Y-You have asked me of my purpose in this unpleasant little inn, but what is yours? All I have done is speak of myself to no good end."

Rafe didn't seem to mind that James had sucked down the last of his ale. "I am here only for the night, too," he said, avoiding the question for the most part. "I am a healer, my lord. That is my gift and my vocation."

James looked at him with interest. "H-Healer, eh?" he said. "A-A physician? A noble profession. But you are too late for all of those gallant lads at Culloden. They could have used you months ago. My brother could have used you months ago. A bayonet to the neck, I was told. Only there is no recovering from that."

Gaira returned to the chamber with Carrie in tow, both of them carrying blankets and pillows. James' drunken chatter ceased at that moment as the women arranged a pallet for him in the corner, next to the hearth. They didn't bring anything for Rafe and when James started to say something about it, the man waved him off and James let the subject drop. If Rafe didn't want a bed, so be it.

Truthfully, James didn't mind sleeping on the floor. He'd slept on worse. He was grateful for the blankets and the fire, and for the company of a rather silent man named Rafe. He'd spoken more of his brother to Rafe than he had spoken to anyone in a very long time and there was something decidedly cathartic about it. But there was also something undeniably depressing, like a stench of tumultuous brotherhood he simply couldn't shake.

A brother he'd not parted on the best of terms with.

He slept.

Part Three

GAIRA

THERE WAS SOMETHING in her face that suggested… shock.

Surprise?

Astonishment?

Rafe saw it in Gaira's face as she'd listened to James drunkenly spout his tale of woe with regard to his relationship with his brother. James had been oblivious to the fact that Gaira had been trying not to be obvious as she listened to him.

But Rafe was aware.

When James finally fell into an inebriated

stupor, Rafe left the chamber in search of the eavesdropping young servant.

Something in her features suggested that she might have known something.

The kitchen was mostly dark at this hour, the only light coming from the wide-mouth hearth that was spitting smoke into the room. As Rafe entered, he spied a big man with a cap on his head bent over a table. Rafe could see that the man was counting money, more than likely the receipts of the day. Rafe moved silently, as he always did, until the man caught movement out of the corners of his eyes and looked up.

"Where did ye come from?" he asked, a mouthful of bad teeth reflecting in the firelight. "I dinna hear ye enter."

Rafe smiled politely. "I did not mean to startle you," he said. "Are you the proprietor?"

The man nodded. "I am Balthazar," he said. "What can I do for ye?"

Rafe looked around the big kitchen to see if there was anyone else in the room that he had missed. "I'm looking for a woman," he said. "She brought food and drink. She also brought…"

Balthazar cut him off. "Oh, *her*," he said. "That's my daughter, Carrie. She's a good lass even if she is a wee bit talkative. Did she tell ye that she's looking for a man tae take her tae London? If she did, then just know I willna let her go. She's been looking for a man tae take her away since she sprouted tits. Eh… I probably shouldna have said that, but ye get my meaning. Ye canna have her."

Rafe was looking at him with a bemused and slightly horrified expression. "I have not had any conversation at length with her," he said hesitantly. "There was another lass with her. Brown-eyed and pretty."

"Ah," Balthazar said knowingly. "That's Gaira. She's a good lass. She's not giddy like Carrie can be. She's got a good head on her shoulders, that one. If ye think she looks different from the rest of the rabble here, she is."

"What do you mean?"

Balthazar leaned back in his chair. "From nobility," he said. "Comes from a family of *mormaer*."

"Rulers?"

"Earldom," Balthazar said. "Her grandfather was the Earl of Forth until the family fell out of favor and their lands taken. Gaira lives with her mother in a home on the edge of town. No menfolk, no armies. Just Gaira and her mother, who cleans chambers for me, although the woman is going tae need more help given the state of my establishment. It looks like we had our very own battle out there in the common room."

Rafe nodded. "I saw," he said. "And that happened only today?"

Balthazar shook his head. "Nay," he said, dragging out the word. "Yesterday we had a war out there. Tore up the room and other chambers as well. We just started picking up the pieces until this happened today. I think I might leave it alone for a few days. Surely someone else is going tae come and try tae tear it up again."

"Why would you say that?"

Balthazar sighed wearily. "'Tis the season for peace and madness," he said. "It seems tae bring out the best and the worst in people. But this year, 'tis particularly bad."

Rafe smiled faintly. "Because it is the first holiday season after the battle at Culloden," he said. "I cannot imagine that those who experienced the battle as you did are finding much peace this season."

Balthazar shook his head, sobering drastically. He suddenly appeared quite weary, as the mere memory was sucking everything out of him.

"It would take a few lifetimes tae overcome what we saw," he said. "We nursed wounded, at least those who could make it here from the field of battle. By the time they reached us, some couldna be helped. Carrie even went tae the battlefield tae look for more wounded, but there were none left. So she collected what possessions she could find and brought them back here so the scavengers wouldna get them. People heard that she was collecting things and some brought her what they'd found."

He trailed off, sadness in his tone, but Rafe was listening intently. "What did you do with all of it?" he asked.

Balthazar lifted a hand in the general direction of the rest of the tavern. "Put it away," he said. "We have a whole chamber full of things from the battle. Someone tried tae destroy it, the same people who ruined the common room yesterday, but the chamber still stands. It still has things from the dead and as long as there is breath in my body, it'll go untouched. Carrie calls it the Chamber of Sorrows. That's what it is, ye know... a place full of sorrow. But it's also a shrine tae the brave dead."

Rafe turned his attention in the direction the old man had indicated. *Chamber of Sorrows*, he thought. A memorial to the dead of Culloden, preserved by an old tavernkeep and his daughter. Rafe thought that perhaps his new friend, James, might find something of his brother there, something from the man that had him so tormented.

But first, he had a woman to see.

"That was kind of you," he said. "Gathering possessions that were important to someone, once. I should like to see them sometime if Carrie will show me, but Gaira... I wish to speak with her.

24

Can you tell me where she is?"

Balthazar allowed himself to reflect on the horrors of Culloden's aftermath for a moment longer before shaking himself, returning his focus to the question at hand.

"She's gone home for the night," he said. "But she just left. If ye hurry, ye might catch her. Her mother's home is down the main road, at the end of town. Ye'll see a two-storied, stone house with a walled yard. 'Tis where Gaira lives."

Rafe thanked him swiftly and dashed out into the night.

The snow was falling lightly and it wasn't difficult to see. Cottages along the avenue were lit from inside, just enough light to see by as Rafe made his way down the avenue, hoping to catch Gaira before she entered her mother's home. But he had a feeling the conversation with Balthazar had cost him time.

Still, it was important he speak with her.

The house Balthazar described came up quickly. There was, indeed, a walled yard, but the wall wasn't any taller than a man's chest. He could see the two-storied home, simple and modest, and faint light emitted from a window on the ground floor. Entering the walled yard, and hoping there weren't dogs to chase him off, he went to the heavily fortified entry door and rapped firmly upon it.

He could hear voices inside. Women's voices.

He rapped again.

"I've come seeking Gaira," he said loudly, hoping they could hear him. "I have no weapons and I mean you no harm. I've come from Balthazar's. He told me where to find Gaira."

More voices. After a moment, someone threw a bolt and the door creaked open. In the dim light beyond, he could see Gaira's suspicious face. Once she got a look at him, however, recognition dawned.

"I know ye," she said, opening the door a little wider. "I served ye food and drink."

Rafe nodded. "You did," he said. "May I come in, please? I'll only stay a moment. I promise that I've not come to harm you. You can see that I have no weapons."

He opened his cloak to show her that he had nothing visible. Gaira inspected him before glancing over her shoulder at something Rafe couldn't see. After a moment, she returned her attention to Rafe and opened the door wider. As he stepped into the warm and stuffy chamber, he could see a woman in the corner with a big ax. Clearly, she was ready to use it if he made the wrong move.

"Thank you for seeing me," he said, keeping his focus on Gaira and not the woman ready to split his skull. "I am not sure how to start this conversation, so I will simply come out with it. You were in the chamber when Worcester was speaking of finding his brother, an officer who perished at Culloden."

Gaira was listening closely but cautiously. "Aye," she said. "I was there."

"You heard the entire conversation."

Gaira wasn't quite sure what he meant. "I heard him speaking," she said. "I dunna know if it was everything he spoke of."

Rafe paused, trying to determine the best way to direct the conversation and not upset her in the process. "As he was speaking, I could see your face," he said. "It seemed to me that Culloden has affected you also. Was I wrong?"

Gaira looked at him for a moment, growing uneasy. "It affected all of us, m'laird," she said. "The battle was a great tragedy."

Rafe could see from the look on her face that he'd hit a nerve. "Balthazar told me about Carrie's Chamber of Sorrow," he said. "He told me that she collected many things from the battle and put them there for safe keeping."

Gaira nodded, averting her gaze as if suddenly unable to look him in the eyes. "I… I know," she said. "I've been in the chamber, many a time."

"Then you know what is in there?"

She nodded.

He hesitated. "Gaira, forgive me for asking,

but have you seen something from Worcester?" he asked, almost gently. "I know you heard Worcester speak of his brother, and it occurred to me that you might have seen something from the English. Perhaps something... belonging to his brother?"

Gaira began to blink rapidly, as if blinking away tears. "I... I dunna know..." she stammered. "There are a great many things in that chamber. Men have been bringing them since the battle ended because they've heard of Carrie's treasures. There are many things there."

"Some from the English?"

"The English were at the battle."

"They were," he agreed. "Only fifty Englishmen lost their lives. Surely something of theirs ended up in that chamber."

"Why should ye ask me? Ask Carrie."

She was growing agitated and he realized he was going to lose her because the woman with the ax was about to chase him out. But he made one last plea.

"Imagine if you were searching for your brother, Gaira," he said, making sure he was close to the door should that ax come hurling at him. "If you know something about Worcester's brother, it would be the merciful thing to tell him. This is the season of our Lord, after all. It is the time when Christ was born and angels walked the earth. If you know something, give Worcester that gift.

Help him find some peace. He needs you."

That was about all Rafe could say because the old woman with the ax had moved out of the shadows and was coming for him. He quickly opened the door and bolted out into the gently falling snow, slamming the door in his wake.

When he was gone, the old woman with the ax threw the bolt on the door before turning to Gaira.

"*Sassenach*," she muttered with distaste. "He's brave coming here tae ask such questions."

Gaira was struggling to compose herself, struggling not to appear too unnerved to her mother, who could be a hard woman at times. She simply wouldn't understand what was in the tender heart of her daughter.

She never had.

"There's a man at the inn who has come tae look for his brother," she said, realizing her voice was trembling. "His brother was killed there."

"English?"

"Aye."

"Then it was God's will," the old woman said. "Send him tae the church in Inverness. 'Tis where they buried them."

Gaira simply nodded. As her mother went to put the ax away, Gaira headed up to her chamber, up the small, spiral stairs and into a room that was dark but for the soft glow of the hearth.

Shutting the door, Gaira stoked the fire to bring a little more light and heat into the chamber before she went to a wardrobe against the wall. Pulling open the sticky door, there were neat rows of clothing folded inside, with still other clothing hanging on pegs on the door and inside the cabinet. It looked like any other wardrobe.

But this one was different.

It was one of the few things passed down by her ancestors, something salvaged from the Earl of Forth's properties and brought to this tiny village on the outskirts of Inverness. This particular wardrobe had a false bottom to store valuables in secret and Gaira opened the trap door that exposed the contents of the secret compartment.

There was only one thing there.

Carefully, Gaira pulled out a tattered, stained haversack. But it wasn't just any haversack – it was one she'd found in Carrie's Chamber of Sorrow, back in the early days when Carrie was still accumulating her collection.

Gaira had been there when the chamber started to gather shields and sabers and the memories of the lost. This particular haversack had come from a local tradesman who'd gone looking for metal to salvage. He'd brought it to Carrie, trading it for some drink and a meal. Carrie went through it for anything valuable before putting it aside with the other haversacks from the nameless, faceless dead. That was when Gaira had found interest in this particular haversack.

It contained letters.

Gaira could read. Her mother had taught her how and she found more interest in the letters of the dead than in their actual possessions. Several of the haversacks contained letters, and she'd read all of them, but this haversack had been different.

Through those carefully scripted letters, a story unfolded.

It was the story of two brothers.

Carefully, she unbuttoned the three brass buttons holding the haversack closed and opened the flap. Inside were bundles of letters wrapped in hemp twine and she pulled out a bundle to look at it.

Fidelis Semper.

Ever Faithful.

It was the motto of the House of de Lohr.

Gaira could hardly believe the man who had written these very letters had come looking for them. Or, more correctly, looking for the man for whom the letters were intended. She hadn't thought much of the British visitor to the inn until he started talking about his missing brother. She listened more carefully. And then, the name…

De Lohr.

Gaira sank to her buttocks, sitting on the floor with the letters clutched to her breast. She had read every single letter, more than once. Something about them spoke to her in a way she couldn't fully grasp and she had stolen the haversack, keeping it hidden away in her chamber. Carrie didn't even know it was missing because she'd taken anything of value out of the haversack and put it aside, but these letters... they were the *only* thing of value as far as Gaira was concerned.

From the words on the yellowed paper, she'd come to know James de Lohr. There were letters written by James when he was a young lad, all the way until most recently before Johnathan went to war. The earlier letters were from a sensitive, somewhat spoiled young boy, upset with the way his brother had spoken to him or made demands of him. It was usually the same thing, fighting over the way Johnathan had behaved or making mention of a speech impediment.

Gaira had heard that for herself.

But that sensitive, somewhat spoiled young boy had grown into a young man who was still quite sensitive and quite brilliant. He had a gift for words, for writing, and she came to understand that it was because he was self-conscious about speaking. It was easier for him to write than it was for him to speak. But the beauty in his words was something that had endeared her to him.

A man she had fallen for, sight unseen.

But he was here now, a faceless fantasy now

come to life.

She could still hardly believe it.

But having heard James speak, she realized there was so much more he didn't know about his brother.

Could she tell him? *Would* she tell him?

Give Worcester that gift. Help him find some peace.

Gaira wondered if she was brave enough to.

Part Four

CARRIE

J AMES AWOKE TO Carrie looking down at him.

Startled, he blinked and instinctively pulled back, bumping his head on the stone wall. Surprised that he had awoken, Carrie jumped back as well.

"I'm sorry, m'laird," she gasped. "Did ye hurt yer head?"

Hand to his head, James frowned as he labored to sit up. "N-No more than it already is," he grumbled, wincing. "W-What are you doing here?"

Carrie's big, green eyes looked at him with concerned. "I came tae see if ye were dead."

"D-Dead?"

"Because ye slept so long. 'Tis midday."

James' eyebrows lifted and he ended up leaning against the wall, rubbing the bump on his head.

"M-Midday, you say?"

"Aye."

He sighed heavily. "I-I'm not dead," he said. "B-But the way my head is throbbing, I surely wish I was."

Carrie retrieved a cup from the table. "Drink this," she said. "It'll help."

He took it, smelled it, and immediately yanked it away from his nose. "B-Bleeding Christ," he muttered. "W-What is that?"

Carrie pushed the cup back towards his mouth. "It'll cure ye," she said. "Drink it quickly. Dunna stop tae taste it; just drink."

James didn't have much choice. She was heavily pushing the cup on him, whatever it was, so he pounded it back like a shot, all in one swallow. But the second the taste hit him, the contents nearly came back up again.

"G-God," he moaned, shoving the cup at her. "What in the hell was in that?"

Carrie set the cup aside, a smile playing on her lips. "Vinegar and eggs."

"*W-What?*"

She nodded. "Vinegar mixed with raw eggs," she said. "It'll cure the pain in yer head. Our customers swear by it."

"O-Or swear *at* it," James mumbled. He wiped at his mouth as if to wipe away the taste and took a deep breath. "W-What does the day look like?"

Carrie went to the only window in the chamber, which was covered with heavy shutters. Unbolting one of them, she pried it open, letting the icy air into the stuffy, smelly chamber.

"More snow from last night, but the sky is clear," she said. Then, she turned to look at him. "So yer brother was at the battle at Culloden, was he?"

He was rubbing his stiff neck at this point, but he glanced at her. "W-Who told you that?"

"Ye did," she said.

"I-I did not."

"Aye, ye did. Do ye not remember?"

Truth be told, James didn't remember a whole lot from last night, but he knew that when he drank, he became rather chatty. He'd give away the secret to the family jewels if he was drunk enough, something his brother often scolded him for. One thing he did remember, however, was the man he'd spoken with the night before and he couldn't help but notice that the man wasn't in the chamber. He seemed to be quite alone this morning but for Carrie.

"A-Aye," he said after a moment. "I suppose I remember."

"And ye asked me what happened tae the dead."

He stopped rubbing his neck. "D-Do you know?"

She nodded. "Mostly," she said. "We're on the road that leads tae the battlefield, ye know. It's two or three days tae the north, but still close enough. Information travels quickly on this road."

"I-I know." When she didn't offer up anything more, he sat forward. "C-Carrie, if you will tell me what you know, I'll make it worth your while. I did not come expecting information for free."

She shook her head. "'Tis not that," she said. "But… many of our lads died there."

"My brother died there."

"Ye dinna come tae dig up the ground, did ye? Because if ye did, I'll not tell ye anything."

James leaned back against the wall, running his fingers through his hair. It was longer, and being that he was blond, people said he had the de Lohr "lion" look. His brother had the look even greater than he did, for Johnathan had the blond mane and the firm jaw. James had more of a refined look, while Johnathan had the look of something that needed to be tamed.

It was a countenance that had ladies eating

out of his hand.

James had never quite mastered that.

"I-I swear to you that I do not intend to go digging up the field of battle," he said sincerely. "A-All I want is to find out what I can about my brother's final resting place. He was with the English and I'm assuming they weren't left on the field of battle to rot. That battlefield is sacred Scots ground and they wouldn't leave the English there. A-Am I correct in that assumption?"

Carrie nodded reluctantly. "T-They took the English tae the church in Inverness," she said. "At least, that's what I was told. But... but I may be able tae help ye before ye go all the way tae Inverness. I have something that I want ye tae see."

She stood up from the chair and James bolted to his feet, probably faster than he should have. The world rocked a bit as he regained his equilibrium. There were two doors in the dingy little chamber – one that opened into the scullery and a second door near the hearth. It was through this door that he followed Carrie, into another dingy chamber with two small beds and a wardrobe that took up most of one wall.

As James watched, Carrie went to one side of the wardrobe and shoved. The furniture apparently wasn't as heavy as it looked because it slid easily across the wooden floor. It was then that James realized the wardrobe was covering yet another door, now partially revealed. Carrie lit a lamp on a nearby table and picked it up.

"Come," she said.

There was an element of mystery as James followed her into the room behind the wardrobe. As Carrie held up the lamp to light the small, dark chamber, his eyes widened.

It was a treasure trove revealed.

Shields, spurs, broken blades, parts of muskets, whole muskets, pistols, coats, ruck sacks, and so much more. The chamber was low-ceilinged, with rough stone walls and the old dirt floor, but it was literally packed to the ceiling with things belonging to men.

To an army.

Armies.

James looked at her in shock.

"W-What *is* this place?" he whispered, awed.

Carrie looked around the chamber. "It belongs tae me," she said softly. "I keep these things safe."

James' sense of astonishment grew. He could see the standards – Wolfe, Barrel, Fleming, Sackville – all of them battalions who had fought at Culloden. There were shoes on the floor, neatly lined up, and on a chest sat a stack of sabers. In the corner, a pile of whole and broken targes caught his attention. Some of them had bloodstains, some of them damaged from the musket ball and cannon fire.

Then, there were the flags.

A Saltire lay torn, with holes in it, and on top of that was a British flag that was equally damaged. James stared at the flags, one atop the other, and the shock he experienced transformed into something horrifying. Although he hadn't been at the battle, he was experiencing it through the eyes of the remains.

The smashed, stained remains that still echoed the sickening sound of battle.

He could hear it.

"O-Oh... God," he muttered. "You went to the battlefield and you scavenged all of this, didn't you?"

Carrie was standing inside the chamber, lamp held high. "Nay," she said firmly. "Not scavenge. Some of these things I brought from the battle-field, but other things I was given. They were brought here for safekeeping. I'm protecting them."

James didn't say anything. He had caught sight of the haversacks and he went to them, a dozen or more piled up. Kneeling down, he picked up the first one and peered into it, poking around.

Carrie came up behind him with the lamp.

"As ye can see, their money is still there, if there was any," she said. "I dinna take their money, but I put any valuables away for safekeeping. I thought that, someday, their kin would come looking for them, so I took these before the scavengers could get tae them. I brought ye here so ye could look through all of this, tae see if there is something of yer brother."

James was on one knee in front of the pile of haversacks. As he looked at them, a lone tear popped from his right eye, falling into the ground. The haversacks were stained with blood, most were badly damaged. He was feeling the concussion of the cannon fire and hearing the wail of the musket balls as they flew over his head. If he closed his eyes, he could feel, and hear, everything. He was in the throes of a battle he'd not attended, but his brother had.

Johnathan had been in the middle of it.

Silently, he moved about the chamber, looking for anything that might have belonged to his brother.

"I've lived in the Highlands all my life," Carrie said, oblivious to his inner turmoil. "I see more of people from all over because of the tavern and I talk tae them. I always thought I understood a great deal, but this battle… I dunna understand it."

James was preoccupied with his hunt. "W-What don't you understand?"

Carrie watched him rifle through a pile of

belts and other leather goods. "The British," she said. "They came here tae destroy our lads once and for all. Men like yer brother... why did they have tae come? I dunna understand the needs of war."

James paused. "T-The needs of war," he repeated the words softly. "T-That is a very good question. My family has been fighting for the King of England since Richard the Lionheart held the throne. He's the one who went to The Holy Land and fought against the savages there. His need was to bring Christianity to those men. Every war has a need."

"But what was this need?"

"T-To put down the Pretender, of course."

"And ye believe he's the Pretender? Or do the English fight because they're told tae, not because they believe in the cause?"

James scratched his head. It was an astute question, one without an easy answer. "I-I cannot speak for others, but I fight because that is what I am trained for," he said quietly. "M-My brother and I come from a long line of soldiers. We fight for our king. It is as simple as that."

"Then yer heart isna in it?"

"M-My heart is never in war. I-I don't think my brother's was, either, which makes his death all the more tragic."

Carrie pondered that. "I suppose I want tae

know what is in the hearts of men who would come tae Scotland and kill our lads."

"I-It was duty, Carrie. N-Nothing more."

Carrie fell silent after that. As she continued to follow him about, trying to be helpful by holding the lamp, James dug through piles of bloodied and dirty possessions. There was a neat pile of redcoats, torn and filthy, but nothing that belonged to his brother. In fact, he didn't see anything familiar until he returned to the pile of sabers that was by the chamber door. They were on a chest and leaning against the wall, some upside-down, and he took a moment to look through them more carefully.

And then, he saw it.

It was upside-down, and partially covered with another saber, but he recognized it right away. The gorgeous hilt and shield-shaped langet, for inside the langet was a lion's head.

De Lohr.

With a gasp, James pulled his brother's sword forth, staring at it for a moment before feeling tears sting his eyes. The physical and emotional reaction was both unexpected and swift, and he clutched the saber to him as the tears silently fell.

It was something of his brother's he'd not expected to find.

"C-Christ," he gasped. "I-It's my brother's sword. It's Johnathan's. Where did you find it?"

Carrie was trying to get a look at it. "I dunna know," she said. "I found some myself, but others were brought tae me. I dunna know where that one came from."

James didn't press her. He held it up, looking at it, inspecting it with shaking hands before once again clutching the hilt to his chest. He was overcome with grief.

"W-Were you holding this when you died, Johnny?" he whispered tightly. "D-Did you really face all of this alone, without me by your side?"

There were no answers to his questions, only the soft darkness of a chamber that was closing in around him. The ghosts of the men who had owned these possessions were coming forth, looking upon him in judgment because he hadn't been at Culloden and he should have been.

God only knew, James had judged himself just as harshly.

"I-I'm sorry, Johnny," he murmured, closing his eyes as tears streamed. "I-I'm sorry I was not there to hold your hand, to lie to you and tell you that you would survive. I'm sorry that my voice, pitiful as it is, was not the last voice you heard in this lifetime, nor my face the last thing you saw. I'm sorry I failed you when you needed me most. God forgive me, I have done nothing but fail you since the day I was born. B-But I have come to take you home and I swear to God I will not leave without you. I will *not* fail you this time."

It was a deeply painful moment as James struggled with his composure. Behind him, he could hear sniffling and he turned to see Carrie weeping into her dirty handkerchief. It was then he realized that this woman, this stranger, had been witness to his most private pain. She'd gathered these souvenirs of war and now she was seeing a reaction to her cultivated collection.

She was seeing the human side of it.

Feeling foolish with his outburst, James wiped his face, clutching the sword so tightly that his knuckles had turned white.

He took a deep breath.

"I-Inverness, you said?" he asked Carrie. "T-That is where the English are buried?"

Carrie nodded, wiping her nose. "Aye," she said. "The Old High Church. They took some of the wounded, too, I heard. Perhaps ye'll find something more of yer brother there."

James looked at the sword in his hand. "I-I have found this," he said. "Y-You cannot know what this means to me. That you took it and did not let the scavengers get to it… I can never thank you enough."

Carrie forced a tremulous smile. "I'm glad ye found it, m'laird."

James was feeling weary, emotional. "A-As am I," he said. "I-It means everything to me and to my mother. But there is something else I seek, something I am sure you have not seen, but I'll ask anyway. A ring with a lion's head – have you seen it?"

Carrie shook her head. "Nay," she said. "If I had, I would tell ye."

"I-It is very valuable."

"I dinna collect these things for profit. I did it because it was the right thing tae do."

He lifted his eyebrows wearily. "F-Forgive me if I've offended you," he said. "A-As I said, I was certain you had not seen it, but I had to ask."

With that, he turned away, clutching his brother's sword in his left hand and moving like a man who was overwhelmed with life. His brother's saber had been found, but that was not where he would stop. Finding the weapon renewed his determination.

Inverness was his next destination.

Part Five

GAIRA

S HE SAW HIM in the snowy livery yard, baggage in hand. He also had a saber with him, something she didn't remember seeing on him when he arrived.

He was leaving.

Gaira stood at the kitchen door as it opened out into the muddy kitchen yard, seeing a portion of the livery from where she stood. She had come to the tavern at her usual time that morning, but James had still been asleep until Carrie went to go wake him a little while ago. Gaira had been busy in the kitchen, but her mind had been on Carrie and James. Truthfully, *only* on James.

Then, she saw him make his way to the livery.

Give Worcester that gift. Help him find some peace.

Those words had been ringing around in her head all night. She had no idea what happened to the tall, pale man who had come to her home to speak to her of the handsome young earl, but he'd departed and now Worcester was leaving as well. If he left, she might never see him again.

He would never know what she knew.

She knew, deep in her heart, that she couldn't let him leave.

Taking a deep breath, she pulled off her apron and left it behind as she ran across the kitchen yard. Since her home wasn't far, it took her little time to cross the muddy road and into the walled yard. The door to the home was unlocked even though her mother wasn't at home, so Gaira hastened to her bedchamber to retrieve the haversack from its secret place.

Even as she held it, her hands were trembling. The contents of the haversack had been her guilty pleasure, and even a large part of her world, for the last several months. Ever since she'd stolen it from Carrie and kept it hidden so she could bask in those letters over and over again. Letters from a sensitive and tormented young man to his equally sensitive and tormented brother.

So much about Johnathan had been different.

So much about James had been deep.

They simply couldn't find a way to connect.

But James had come for his brother and it wasn't fair for her to keep the letters any longer. She never really thought this moment would come, and she was going to have to explain to him why she had kept them this long, but she would have to face him with what she'd done. Knowing James as she did through his beautiful letters, she felt as if she knew him well. It was strange knowing a man well she'd never actually met.

Until now.

Those letters didn't belong to her, after all.

They belonged to a beleaguered young earl.

Clutching the haversack to her chest, she wrapped herself back up in her simple shawl, one that wasn't nearly enough against the icy temperatures, and ran back across the road and into the livery.

As she entered the yard, she saw James standing just outside of the stable as the groom prepared his mount. It was a long-legged bay thoroughbred, a beautiful and expensive animal. The groom led the animal over to the trough to water the steed while he finished with the tack, leaving James standing by himself.

Gaira's stomach was twisting with nerves as

she came up behind him, studying his broad back and wide shoulders. It was the James from the letters, a sweet and angsty young man who was better in the flesh than she could have ever imagined.

"M'laird?" she said, a little breathlessly.

He turned to her and Gaira took a good, long look at his face in the sunlight. Blond, well-built, and excruciatingly handsome, he was quite the perfect young lord.

His sky-blue eyes fixed expectantly on her.

"W-What is it?" he asked.

Her heart began to flutter. "I… I heard ye speaking tae yer companion last night," she said, stepping into the livery. It was quieter in there, out of the elements. "Ye came seeking yer brother."

James' focus had followed her as she'd walked around him and entered the stable. But with the mention of last night's legendary conversation, he grunted and rolled his eyes.

"I-It seems that everyone in this wretched place knows about that now," he said. "D-Don't worry, I'm leaving. It seems that Inverness may hold more answers for me."

Gaira could see how weary he was.

But she was about to change that.

"Perhaps ye'll find yer brother's body there," she said. "But I have his heart here."

With that, she unwounded her shawl to reveal

the haversack clutched to her chest. James wasn't certain what he was looking at, at first, but when she held it up to him and he recognized it, all of the color drained from his face. His mouth popped open and something of a groan escaped.

"M-My God," he said hoarsely. "I-It's his haversack. This is my brother's haversack."

Gaira nodded, carefully depositing it into his trembling hands. "It is," she said. "Last night, when I heard ye speak about yer brother, I was certain that this belonged tae ye. Ye see, I've had it for a long while and I… well, I have much tae say about it before ye go. Would ye give me a moment of yer time, m'laird?"

James was unbuttoning the haversack with shaking hands. In fact, he could hardly get it open, but he wasn't so singularly focused that he didn't hear Gaira's soft plea. He nodded so vigorously that his hair wagged about.

"O-Of course," he said, reaching out to grasp her by the arm. "C-Come and tell me everything you know. What is your name again?"

"Gaira, m'laird," she said. "Gaira Dunmore."

"G-Gaira," he repeated, clutching the haversack as he led her away from the livery entry and into a quiet area near the stalls. "I-I remember you. I helped you and Carrie escape the battle in the common room yesterday."

Gaira nodded. "Ye did," she said. "I'm sorry I

dinna thank ye for it yet. There's not been the opportunity."

"I-I know," James said. Then, he dropped to one knee and set the haversack down on a pile of clean hay so he could poke around in it. "C-Christ, I can hardly believe you found this. Did you know my brother, then? How did you come by it?"

Gaira watched him pull out a stack of carefully-tied letters. James' question was one with a complicated answer. She was afraid if she didn't tell him everything, and tell him quickly, that she would lose him to the excitement and relief of finding his brother's haversack. He might even chase her away so he could be alone with his brother's memories. Already, she could see that he was distracted with it.

Taking a deep breath, she summoned her courage.

"The haversack was brought tae Carrie by a man who was scavenging the battlefield for metal," she said steadily. "Carrie put it in her chamber with all of the other things she had collected, and as I had done with others, I looked through them. Only this haversack was different. Ye asked me if I knew yer brother, m'laird, and the answer is that I do. I know ye, too. Did ye know he kept the letters ye wrote tae him since the time ye were a young lad until recently?"

James' hands were still trembling, but his

initial shock was being overtaking by some confusion. *Bewilderment.* He fingered through the stack in his hand only to realize something.

"B-But… but some of these are very old," he said, peering at one. "M-My God, these are all from me."

Gaira knelt down beside him. "They are," she said softly, looking at his face as he unfastened the hemp string. "M'laird… I read through every single letter. Everything ye wrote tae yer brother. Because of the catch in yer speech, ye wrote him letters when ye quarreled because when ye became upset, the catch grew worse and it was difficult for ye tae speak."

He stopped pawing and looked at her. "H-How did you know that?"

Gaira found herself staring into eyes that were as beautiful as a new day. "I told ye," she said, a hint of a smile on her lips. "Because I read every single letter. Did ye know that yer brother replied tae every letter ye ever wrote him?"

James' gaze was riveted to her. "H-He did not," he said. "H-He never wrote to me."

Gaira's smile broke through as she reached into the haversack and pulled out another pile of letters. She held them up between them.

"He did," she said. "I dunna know why he never gave them tae ye, but for every letter ye wrote him, he wrote one in return. They're all here, in order. I put them in order of the date, or at least as close as I could get."

James' mouth opened in astonishment as he took the stack from her, looking at it. It was a shocking revelation. After a moment, he swallowed hard.

"Y-You read all of these?" he asked.

Gaira's smile faded. "I did," she said. "Believe me when I tell ye that when I first found the haversack, I only intended tae read one or two, tae find out who the sack belonged tae. That was my original intention and I swear that tae ye. But the more I read, the more I wanted tae read. I've read those letters so many times that I've nearly memorized them."

James set down the stack of the letters he had written so that he could focus on the ones Johnathan had written to him. But he made no move to untie the string. He simply sat there and looked at them.

"I-If what you say is true, they were not meant for you," he said after a moment.

She averted her gaze, ashamed. "I know," she said. "I dinna mean tae intrude, but I couldna help myself. There's such a beautiful story in those letters."

He snorted. "I-I am not sure that's possible," he said. "A-Anything I wrote is drivel. I-I don't even know what my brother's letters say."

"Ye need tae read them."

"I-I am not sure I can."

"Why not?"

He glanced at her. "I-I am not sure why I should say that to you," he said. "W-We are strangers, you and I. This is a private family matter and you surely would not care."

Gaira laughed softly. "We are *not* strangers," she said. "I know ye better than I've known most people in my life and I've never even met ye until now. Do ye want tae know what I know of ye? I know that ye're brilliant and witty and sensitive, things ye thought yer brother believed were weaknesses, but I tell ye it's not true. He dinna think that."

"N-Now you're making up lies."

She shook her head firmly. "Indeed, I'm not," she insisted. "Ye can read them for yerself. There's a letter yer brother wrote tae ye six years ago after ye attended a fete given by a family named Summerlin. There was a young woman ye had yer eye on but when ye spoke tae her, she shunned ye. Ye ran off and no one could find ye for two days and when your brother finally found ye drowning yer sorrows at a coach inn, ye scolded him and told him tae go away. Do ye remember that incident?"

James was looking at her dubiously. "I-I do, in fact," he said quietly. "T-The young woman was

A-Amy Summerlin."

"Of Blackstone Castle."

When he realized she really *did* know the situation, he became less doubtful. "S-She pretended to be interested in what I had to say when, in fact, I later heard her mocking my speech with her friends and laughing. I-I was humiliated and left the party."

Gaira nodded her head in the direction of the letters he held in his hand. "Ye never let yer brother tell ye that he had avenged ye," she said gently. "In one of those letters, he tells ye that he corresponded with Amy for six months after the incident, pretending tae be a great duke, and promised he'd call upon her. On the appointed day, he never showed up and left Amy greatly humiliated."

James looked at her, incredulous. "I-I think I heard of that," he said. "M-My mother spoke of Amy Summerlin being made a fool of and how she was the laughingstock of her social circle. A-And you're telling me that *my* brother did that?"

"He did."

"For me?"

"For ye. The man had a naughty streak in him tae be sure."

James had known that for the most part. But the fact that his brother had avenged him in a situation where he'd blamed his brother for his problems was astonishing. But that astonishment was coupled with growing remorse.

"H-He tried to speak to me about it, a few times, but I shut him off," he said, thinking back to that time. "I-I never let him speak of it, so he never told me what he'd done."

Gaira watched the regret ripple across his face. "He wrote ye a letter about it instead," she said. "Ye wrote tae him because ye couldna speak, and he wrote tae ye because ye wouldna *let* him speak. I think ye should read the letters, m'laird. I think yer brother was a different man than ye knew."

James sank down to his buttocks, still clutching the stack of bound letters. There was so much remorse and angst in his heart to realize that Johnathan had written him so many letters he never gave to him.

The question was why.

He suspected he knew.

"W-Was I really so difficult to communicate with?" he muttered aloud. "W-Why would he write all of these and never give them to me? Was he so afraid of my reaction?"

Because he sat down, Gaira sat down. "I dunna have the answers ye seek, m'laird, but I'll tell ye what I think," she said. "Yer brother was a proud man. As his younger brother, ye're supposed tae look up tae the man and believe him perfect. Isna that what younger brothers do for the older ones?"

James leaned back against the wall of the stall, his attention returning to the lovely woman with the big, brown eyes. "A-Aye," he said. "B-But I always looked up to him."

"He knew," Gaira said honestly. "And I think that perhaps he thought it would show weakness tae give ye the letters he'd written. Ye'd see that he was a man of flesh and bone and feeling, not the perfect earl who was anything but perfect."

James' brow furrowed. "S-So you're saying that he was embarrassed to give them to me?"

Gaira shook her head. "Not embarrassed," she said. "But a man has his pride. I think pride kept him from showing ye that he was just as sensitive as ye are. Now that he's gone... he knew that the letters would make their way back tae ye and that ye would read him. There's a letter he wrote tae ye the night before the battle at Culloden, in fact. If ye dunna read the others, just read that one. Yer brother took the time tae write it, so it's important that ye do."

James stared at her a moment and Gaira could see the thoughts churning behind those brilliant eyes. With a faint sigh, he looked to the stack of letters in his hand.

"H-Here?" he said. "I-In this group?"

Gaira nodded. "'Tis right on the top," she said. "I organized them by date, so the last one is on the top."

James looked at it. He wasn't certain that he was strong enough to read it, but something inside him was pining for it. The last words from his brother, perhaps a hint of approval or a glimmer of hope for those he left behind.

This was what he'd come for, after all.

Something of his brother.

He untied the twine and retrieved the letter on the top.

The paper was yellowed, the seal broken. It was dog-eared on one side as he opened it up to see the familiar handwriting. It was like a dagger to his heart simply to see Johnathan's carefully-scripted letters, but he fought the grief it provoked.

He continued.

My dearest James –

If you are reading this, I'm assuming that I did not survive the battle. I'm further assuming that some kind Scots family has sent you my possessions, such as they are, and that you realize you are now the Earl of Worcester. Although I am no expert on the post, as I suspect I did not do our family justice, I have no doubt that you will be a much finer earl than I ever was. How do I know this?

Because I know you.

When Mother was pregnant with you, I was a tiny lad, but I knew enough to know that I wanted a brother. I remember praying aloud for a brother and the priest would slap me on the head in the midst of my prayers because of it. That old bastard, Father Bernardo. I know you remember him. I think he slapped you a time or two, also.

And then you were born and I had a brother. Mother would leave you in your bed to cry at night and I would climb in with you to comfort you. I know you do not remember that, but I did. I would lay beside you and tell you what great things we would do together, the both of us. I was convinced we would ride side by side into battle in the morning, vanquish the enemy, and be in the tavern drinking wine by evening. I was convinced we would be inseparable.

I think, in a way, we are.

In my possessions, you'll find a stack of letters that you wrote to me. Every single letter you ever wrote to me. I have always kept them with me, even on a battle match. There was one in particular that I kept in a pocket next to my heart because it meant a great deal to me. When I came to Culloden without you, the letters came with me. Whether or not you knew it, you were by my side with every step because I knew that no matter what happened, you would be there for me in spirit if not in presence. Those letters are you, even more than if you were with me in the flesh. In them, you have entrusted me with your fears and hopes and insecurities. I take that trust very seriously.

James, I know I have not been the easiest man to know. I can be aloof. I can be quick to temper. I was always jealous of you and the freedom you had, unencumbered with the de Lohr expectations as I was. You were young and brilliant and your laughter... James, I can still hear it. Your laughter is so easy. I don't know how you do it and I always envied it so. But you are also annoying and insufferable at times and sometimes I want to kick you squarely in the fart hole.

Still, you are my brother and I love you.

I know I never told you that, but I do. I always have. Tomorrow, we are facing six thousand rabid Scots and their allies and although we are better armed and better prepared, there is still a chance I will not make it out of this alive. If I do not, I want you to know that it has been a privilege being your brother. I could not have asked for a greater honor. You will be standing beside me tomorrow as I fight the enemy and if I should fall, know that you will be among my final thoughts.

James, I have always adored you and reproach myself most stringently for never telling you so. But I know that my death will be quite devastating to you and as the reverend prayed for the regiment tonight, I prayed that God would send a guardian angel to watch over you after I am gone. I suppose that I was your guardian angel while on earth, but after I am gone, I pray another will take my place.

Do not grieve overly for me. Do not let Mother grieve overly. Take care of her and of yourself, and I wish you joy and happiness all your life. You are my brother, James, and most worthy of the de Lohr name. I have no final wish or instructions except for one – there are many brave men who will fight tomorrow and I consider it an honor to serve with them. Bring my body home, if it is possible, but leave something of me with my men in the place we have fallen. Not everyone will have the

opportunity to return home, so leave some-
thing of me behind to watch over them.
Your mercy is appreciated.

Your loving brother,
John

Tears were running down James' face as he finished. Still holding the letter, he put a hand over his face, giving himself the luxury of indulging in his grief if only for a brief moment. He pictured his brother, writing the letter by candlelight on the eve of a great battle. There was no fear conveyed in the letter, no cowardice or remorse. Simply a man wanting to ensure his affairs were in order and that his brother, the most important person in his life, understood what was in his heart.

He had been right.

James *was* devastated.

"I'm sorry if this has reopened a wound that was trying tae heal," Gaira whispered, breaking into his thoughts. "But I saw the letter and I knew that ye should, too."

James wiped at his face quickly, struggling to compose himself. "Y-You were correct," he said. "I-I am glad I saw it. I only wish... well, my brother and I were not the type to speak affection-ately to each other. We could laugh together, drink together, and argue quite well, but when it came to speaking of our feelings... it simply wasn't done.

T-That is why this letter means so much to me."

Gaira smiled timidly. "I am glad."

There was so much more she wanted to say to him, so much that wouldn't come. Now simply didn't seem like the right time. Before her was the man she'd fallen in love with through his letters but, at the moment, this was not about her or her feelings. This was about James and the loss of a brother.

She didn't feel right saying anything more.

She had done what she'd come to do.

"I… I suppose ye'll be leaving now," she said. "I've heard they buried English officers in Inverness, so perhaps that's where yer brother is. I do wish ye well, m'laird."

She started to stand up, but James stopped her. "W-Wait," he said. "P-Please… wait. I am coming to think that without you, none of this would have been possible."

Gaira paused, realizing that she was close to tears at the thought of leaving those letters behind.

Leaving James behind.

"I'm sure someone would have found them and sent them tae ye," she said. "The Highlands are full of good people, in spite of what the English think."

James was looking at her closely, as if seeing her through new eyes. "P-Perhaps someone would have," he said. "B-But it's equally possible they would have ended up in a hearth somewhere, burned to ashes, and I would have never known what you have been able to give me. It is the greatest kindness anyone has ever bestowed upon me."

Gaira was trying hard not to weep so she lowered her gaze. "Ye're welcome," she said tightly. "As I said, I came tae know ye and yer brother very well. Ye deserve tae have peace between ye."

"I-It is most thoughtful of you to say so," he said, eyeing her. "B-But why do you seem so troubled now?"

Gaira couldn't help it; she broke down in tears. "It's foolish and it shouldna matter," she said. "I'm only a serving wench at a place called Balthazar's where patrons piss on the floor and try tae pinch my backside. I'm no one."

James could see that she was upset and his focus shifted from his own grief to the woman's obvious distress. "Y-You are wrong," he said quietly. "Y-You are the woman who brought my brother back to me. That makes you very special."

Her head snapped up and she looked at him, wishing with all her heart that his statement was true in a romantic sense. That wish removed any sense of restraint as she spoke. She figured that she'd never see the man again, so whatever she said was of little matter.

But she had to say it.

"I've lived my entire life in this dingy little village, with no excitement, no prospects, and no hope," she said. "But my family wasna always impoverished. My grandfather was the Earl of Forth, a great advisor tae King James until he fell out of favor by taking one of the king's mistresses as his own. My family was stripped of everything and we came here tae live, far away from king and court. My grandfather and father were learned men, so they eked out a life here, but when they died, it was only me and my mother and we do what we can tae survive."

James was listening intently. "T-Then you're the heiress to the Earldom of Forth?"

Tears were falling faster than she could wipe them away. "If it still belonged tae my family, aye," she said. "I just thought ye should know that, once, our family fortunes were much as yer family's. We were powerful and wealthy. The earldom had been in our family for centuries and it was taken away in the blink of an eye. I was educated by my grandfather, so I'm not like the other women in this village. I'm different. 'Tis a difficult existence here, much like yer own existence with yer brother. It is... complicated. 'Tis clear by yer letters that ye never felt as if ye fit in, or were worthy, and that's something I can relate tae. I... I suppose in a sense, that's why I felt drawn tae ye both through those letters. But I was drawn tae ye most of all."

His expression softened. "W-Why me?"

She shrugged, unable to look at him. "Because ye're tender," she said. "The things ye wrote tae yer brother speak of a tender heart, a dreaming heart, and of a man who wants tae do right in life. So many men are hardened and cruel, but ye… ye have a soul. Ye've had challenges, but ye've not let them define ye. Do ye want tae know the truth? Yer letters took me out of my hellish existence and, for a moment, I could be by the side of a man who tried tae live the life he was born tae live. I dunna know if that makes sense, but it's the truth. I fell in love with ye and I dunna even know ye, but now that I've met ye, I feel as if I've known ye all my life. I wasna going tae give those letters back because they were so important tae me, but I see now that they're even more important tae ye. I'm sorry I kept them as long as I did and I pray ye can forgive me."

She was looking down at the straw as she finished, preparing for the response sure to come. He would probably thank her for her candor and leave just as fast as he could. Only a madwoman would declare her love for a man she'd only come to know through letters.

But something strange happened.

Suddenly, he was sitting next to her and his

fingers were under her chin, lifting her face to his. Gaira found herself looking into eyes the color of the sky, the slightly-bearded face creased into a smile. For a moment, he simply looked at her before kissing her gently on the cheek.

"L-Lady Gaira," he addressed her formally, as would have been her right as an heiress. "T-The fact that the letters between my brother and me mean so much to you tells me that you are a woman of great depth and understanding. You knew what I needed when I did not even know. I feel that it would only be right to allow me to come to know you as you have come to know me. My brother said that he prayed for a guardian angel to watch over me. Do you think he meant you?"

She flushed a dull red, her heart thumping so forcefully against her chest that she could hardly breath. "Probably not," she said, fighting off a grin. "I've never been called an angel before. A devil, perhaps, but not an angel."

He smiled because she was. "I-I will call you an angel," he said softly. "Y-You have become mine by reuniting me with my brother's belongings."

"But… but I should have done it sooner."

"I-If you had simply sent them to me, I would not have had the honor of meeting you."

There was that sweet man, the one she'd come

to know in the letters. As she had told him, he had a tender side.

"Then perhaps everything happens for a reason," she said. "Perhaps the reason was so we could speak."

"I-I believe so," he said. "A-And I believe something else."

"What?"

"T-That you should come to Inverness with me," he said. "A-After all, it seems to me that you have almost as much invested in this situation as I do. You read Johnny's letters and you know the man, as you've said. Would you like to see this through? I am going to find the man in those letters you so carefully kept."

Gaira was nodding her head before he even finished. "I would," she said, incredulous that he should even ask. "Oh, I would!"

James took his hand off her chin, his eyes glimmering with mirth. "I-I am assuming that your mother would not be too keen on you accompanying me to Inverness, unchaperoned," he said. "I-I would, of course, give you my word that I will behave respectfully and politely, but I would hazard to guess that your mother might not believe the word of a Sassenach."

He said it with the perfect Gaelic inflection and Gaira grinned. "I'm a wicked lass for saying this, but she doesna have tae know."

He cocked an eyebrow. "Y-You would lie to her?"

She shrugged. "Sometimes, I sleep at the tavern, in Carrie's chamber," she said. "Especially when it's cold and we have an early morning the next day. My home is across the road, so 'tis not far, but sometimes it's easier – and warmer – tae sleep in Carrie's chamber. There have been times when I've not been home for a week."

"A-And your mother does not miss you?"

The warm inflection on her face faded. "My mother and I dunna have a close relationship," she said. "She goes about her business and I go about mine, although she does clean at the tavern once in a while. I'll simply tell her she's not needed and tell Balthazar she canna come, so she willna know I'm not there."

She sounded confident, but James was still dubious. "I-It is at least two days to Inverness and two days back," he said. "And the weather is snowy. Are you certain you can do this?"

The warmth was back as she looked at him. "'Tis for Laird Johnathan, after all," she said quietly. "I wouldna miss this for the world."

Within the hour, James and Gaira were heading north, along the road to Culloden.

Part Six

INVERNESS

The Old High Church

JAMES LOOKED AT the man in shock.

"Y-*You*?" he said. "I-I was wondering what happened to you, but now I find you here? In Inverness?"

Rafe had been standing at the entry to the Old High Church that had stood for centuries. The brown stones and high tower faced out over the River Ness, guarding the city both literally and figuratively. It was the spiritual center of the town, but it also served as a prison. Some dark things had happened within the walls of the old building.

Rafe stepped forward, greeting James amiably.

"I knew you would be coming here," he said. "The English dead were buried here, so it was a natural assumption. I came ahead of you. I thought I would help you look for your brother."

James had been on the road for almost three days. The snows hadn't returned, but the roads themselves had been in bad shape. More than that, he'd taken it slowly for Gaira's sake. Standing behind James, she was bundled up in one of his coats against the icy weather.

Hearing Rafe's explanation, James' surprise turned to confusion.

"Y-You thought to…?" he repeated. "B-But why should you do that? Although I appreciate your initiative, my brother's fate is not your concern. Surely you have better things you could be doing."

Rafe shook his head, motioning him and Gaira into the church, which wasn't much warmer than it was outside, but at least it was out of the elements.

"I told you that I am a healer," he said. "This is where I am meant to be at the moment. I came ahead and made some inquiries about Johnathan de Lohr and I believe I found someone who can help you."

James' features registered shock. "Y-You did?"

he said. "*H-Here*?"

Rafe nodded. "As I said, the English were brought here after the battle," he said. "Wounded, prisoners, and dead. All of them were brought here. The battlefield is quite close, in fact. You passed it on your way into town."

James scratched his head, turning to look out into the churchyard as if to see the battlefield beyond. A chill ran over him. "I-I was not aware."

"It is true," Rafe said. "But I spoke to a priest at length here when I arrived. He told me that the British army brought the dead and wounded here and then executed the Jacobite prisoners. If you look into the southeast corner of the churchyard, you will see a mass grave."

James was starting to pale, his breathing deepening when he realized what Rafe was telling him. "M-My brother is in a mass grave?" he clarified. "I-Is that what you are saying?"

Rafe held up a finger, begging patience. "Wait," he said. "Let me find the priest who knows. I shall return quickly."

With that, he wandered off into the dim church, leaving James standing in the entry, feeling as if he'd just been kicked in the gut. He caught movement out of the corners of his eyes, knowing it was Gaira but afraid to look at her.

Afraid he might break down if he did.

He hadn't come this far to discover his brother's remains were jumbled up with a bunch of strangers.

"I'd heard the same thing," Gaira said softly, putting a gentle hand on his arm. "I dinna want tae tell ye. I dunna know it for certain, but word travels. We had heard the English executed prisoners here and buried their dead."

"B-But they wouldn't have buried them with the prisoners."

"Nay."

"D-Does that mean all of the English are in a mass grave, then?"

"Perhaps the priests can tell ye the truth."

Her voice was soft, lilting. *Comforting.* Funny how he couldn't remember when she hadn't been around him somehow – beside him, in front of him, behind him. The past three days with Gaira had been some of the most unusual and important of his young life. As she stood next to him, he put a big arm around her shoulders and pulled her against him.

He drew strength from her.

In fact, she had become so much more to him than a woman who had read his letters and it had all started with this journey. Gaira had been an ideal traveling companion – never complaining, keeping up a steady stream of conversation to make the travel pass more pleasantly. The days had been long and the nights has been...

interesting.

Though James had kept his promise and had behaved like a gentleman, by the second night, they were far too comfortable sleeping in the same room with each other. The first night they'd stopped at an inn, which had been full because of a large family traveling south. Their horses crowded the livery and they even had a carriage that had been parked in the yard. James had managed to negotiate a small bed in the servants' quarters for Gaira, but he ended up sleeping on the bench of the coach because there simply wasn't any other place.

Somewhere in the middle of the night, however, Gaira had come outside with a pillow and two blankets she'd stripped off her rented bed and found him. He'd slept upright against the side of the carriage with a pillow between him and the cab wall, while she'd slept on the bench beside him, her head in his lap.

It wasn't exactly proper, but it had been warm and there had been a great comfort in the fact that they were in the same spot. James, in particular, felt comforted that she wasn't out of his sight. It was odd how attached he'd become to her even in the short time he had known her. They'd left at dawn the next morning after breaking their fast, continuing on as far as they could until they were forced to seek shelter because the night had been so cold.

The second night had been spent on the floor of a farmhouse, in front of the hearth, surrounded by the family's dogs. James had awoken with his arm wrapped around a snoring hound and Gaira had awoken surrounded by dogs who had slept up against her for warmth. It hadn't been the most comfortable sleep, but it had made for a great story.

And now, they were in Inverness.

"James?" she said softly. "Did ye hear me?"

She'd began calling him James yesterday. No longer "m'laird" because, frankly, they were beyond that. He didn't like to hear her address him so formally, so he had asked her to call him James.

She had complied.

As he heard her softly uttered words, he was lashed back to the painful world of reality, a world where his brother was dead and now possibly in a common grave. The impact of it cut through him like a knife.

"I-I heard you," he said after a moment. "I-I suppose we shall discover the truth, but I pray that my brother did not end up in a grave with other dead. He did not deserve that."

Gaira's left arm was around his waist and he felt her squeeze. "Dunna give up hope."

James paused, his thoughts turning from his

brother to the tall, pale stranger who seemed so determined to help him.

"W-What I would like to know is why Rafe came," he said. "I-I seem to remember him asking me if there was anything he could do to help me find Johnny, but I did not expect him to go out of his way to do it."

Gaira held his hand tightly. "'Tis a rare man who would be so kind and helpful," she said. "He's a wanderer. I dunna want tae say that he has nothing better tae do, but he doesna seem tae. Perhaps he is looking for a purpose."

James turned to look over his shoulder at her. "H-Helping a man he does not know?"

"Helping a man who needs it."

She had a point. James squeezed her shoulders affectionately and returned his focus to the church, watching for Rafe's return.

It wasn't long in coming.

Rafe emerged from the darkness with a small man at his side. Clad in a rough woolen coat and breeches, his hair cut short against his skull, the man came into the light, his gaze fixed on James. Before James could say a word, the man spoke quietly.

"Ye have his look," he said quietly. "Ye have his eyes."

James eyed him curiously. "W-Who?"

"Yer brother," the man said. Then, he shook

himself. "Forgive me. I am Reverend Essich. I… I simply canna believe that ye came, m'laird."

James stared at him a moment before taking a deep, steadying breath. "You knew my brother?"

Reverend Essich nodded. Then, he motioned to James. "Come," he said. "Quickly."

James followed, pulling Gaira with him. Rafe walked alongside as they followed Reverend Essich into a small alcove off the main sanctuary. It was private here, the stone-cold darkness pierced by banks of prayer candles.

Reverend Essich cleared his throat softly.

"Eight months ago, those loyal to Stuart were executed by the English out in the churchyard," he said. "Though their cause has greatly died away, there still may be some who would like to see an Englishman dead because of it. Ye took a risk coming here, m'laird."

James nodded. "I-I know," he said. "B-But I have come looking for my brother. It seems to me that you know of him."

Essich nodded. "I do," he said, glancing at Rafe, who nodded encouragingly. "But when he came here, I dinna know his name. When yer friend told me that ye were looking for a man who had been bayonetted through the neck, I thought it might be him and now that I see ye, I know that ye are his brother because ye look just like him. I never even knew his name."

"J-Johnathan," James said without hesitation. "J-Johnathan de Lohr, Earl of Worcester."

Essich smiled faintly, revealing yellowed teeth. "Worcester," he repeated. "The man was nobility."

"He came from a great line of soldiers."

The reverend nodded. "No doubt," he said. "Yer friend says that ye seek the truth about him. I was here on that terrible day when the English were brought here. My fellow brothers and I fought tae save those we could, but in yer brother's case, it was of no use."

James braced himself. "T-Tell me, please," he said. "T-tell me everything you know."

Essich began to wring his hands in a nervous gesture. "I want ye tae know we tried very hard, m'laird."

"I-I understand."

Essich sighed faintly, hoping that was the truth. He hoped the man really did understand because he had much to say.

"The English were brought here by the wagonload," he said. "There were dead and dying men on the wagons, all piled in together. My fellow parishioners and I separated the dead from the dying as Cumberland's men took the Jacobite prisoners and executed them in the churchyard. We could hear the muskets firing regularly. Meanwhile, a group of prisoners had been forced tae dig their own mass grave in the corner of the churchyard."

It was cold-blooded, but such were the perils of war. It didn't usually bother James, but with his brother involved, he was feeling quite emotional about the whole situation.

"G-Go on," he said.

Essich continued. "We thought yer brother was dead when he was brought here, but he wasna," he said, watching James close his eyes tightly. "He dinna die on the field of battle if that's what ye were told. He was brought here in a pile of men and when we realized he was alive, we quickly took him away and put him in the dormitory with the other wounded."

James sighed heavily and hung his head, slumping against the wall behind him. As Gaira and Rafe and Essich looked on with concern, the reverend continued quickly.

"Yer brother had taken a bayonet through the neck," he said. "I dunna know how he survived as long as he did, but he was a strong man because he lived for a full night after he was brought here, and during that night, he never awoke. I made him as comfortable as I could, m'laird."

James had a lump in his throat as he listened. "H-He never regained consciousness?"

Essich shook his head. "Nay," he said. "There were times when I thought he might, but he never did. He wasna alone when he died, if that's of some comfort tae ye. I was with him. I said a prayer for him."

James could feel the tears but he fought them. This was perhaps the best ending he could have hoped for, considering the circumstances. "I-I am grateful," he said. "W-What... what did you do with him?"

"We buried the dead on the other side of the church, opposite the churchyard," Essich said. "Yer brother was buried in his own grave, dressed in the clothing he was wearing, but before we buried him, I removed what possessions he had in the hopes that I could discover who he was."

James was losing the battle against the tears. "What did you find?"

The reverend dug into a pocket of his thread-bare coat and pulled forth a meager handful of things. One looked like it was a folded document of some kind, while there were two other items that became evident when Essich opened his hand and extended it to James. The first thing James saw was the Eardley Norton pocket watch that Johnathan always carried, one that had belonged to their father.

The second thing was the ring.

Ruby eyes glimmered weakly in the candle-light.

"G-God," he gasped, grabbing the ring. "Y-You have it. The ring; *you have it*!"

Essich nodded. "The only thing inscribed on it was *Fidelis Semper*," he said. "Had there been a name, I might have been able tae find ye, but there wasna. Not on the watch and not even on the letter."

James was still reeling over the reclamation of the de Lohr ring. The relief he felt was indescribable, the family heirloom that thankfully wasn't lost as they'd all feared. Now, he had it, and it was his. He slipped it on his finger as he looked up, seeing that Essich was extending the folded paper to him. Hesitantly, he took it.

"H-He had a letter on him?" he asked.

"Aye," Essich nodded. "From someone named James. I found it in a chest pocket, right against his heart."

With the ring on his finger and the watch in one hand, James looked at the letter, feeling the impact of the reverend's words. It was just as Johnathan's letter had told him, how he kept a certain letter close to his heart in battle.

There was one in particular I kept in a pocket next to my heart because it meant a great deal to me.

Swallowing hard, James opened it up to see which letter it was that meant so much to Johnathan. The first thing he saw was a childish scrawl and he knew that it was a letter written by a very young boy. He recognized his own writing.

Lifting it into the light, he began to read.

You are a very mean boy, Johnny.

I want to cut you with my saber and slash you and kill you. If I sound like a Billy goat, then you look like a horse's arse and I don't care if you tell Mummy. You say very mean things to me and I don't care because I am going to kill you. Someday you will be dead and I will be happy. I will draw a picture of me laughing and when you are in the ground, I hope the worms eat your eyeballs. Then I will dig you up and put more worms on you. When you go to heaven, God will see all of the worms in your eyeballs and when I go to heaven, I will see them also. Wait for me when you get to heaven so I can see the worms. If you do not wait for me, I shall be very angry.

Your brother who hates you,
James

Startled by the petulant message in a letter that Johnathan should keep so close to him, James started to laugh. He laughed so hard that tears streamed down his face, but these were tears of delight. That his brother had kept that querulous, silly letter with him, keeping it close to his heart through the years, meant the world to him. It literally meant everything. It was incredibly representative of their childhood, but it was also representative of the bond they shared throughout the insults and bad feelings and torment. It began to occur to James why Johnathan had kept the letter so close.

Wait for me when you get to heaven.

God... so ridiculous, yet so poignant. Johnathan kept a young boy's plea close to his heart because it spoke of James' true adoration for the brother he very much loved.

When he faced battle, that little request had fortified him.

"What does it say?" Gaira asked timidly. "Will ye tell me?"

James was still chuckling. "H-Here," he said, handing it to her. "Y-You can see for yourself."

Gaira took it and read through it, giggling as she came to the end. "Did ye really send such nasty things tae yer brother?" she gasped. "Ye were a naughty lad."

James nodded, taking it from her and carefully folding it. "I-I was," he said. "A-And he loved me for it, so I suppose I wasn't as naughty as I thought. To see that this silly little letter meant something to him... it is a feeling I cannot begin to describe. All I know is that I love it."

Gaira smiled at him and he winked at her

before returning his attention to the reverend. When he looked at the man, his chuckles started anew.

"I-I am the James of that letter, as you may have guessed," he said. "I-I wrote that letter to my brother when I was around six or seven years of age, I believe, and he was nearing twelve. We had quarreled because he told me that I sounded like a goat when I spoke. I'd forgotten that I'd even written him that letter. How surprising to find that it meant so much to him."

Essich was smiling, mostly because he was pleased that something in this horrific circumstance had brought James pleasure.

"The bond between brothers is unique and powerful," he said. "It would seem that ye and yer brother shared that bond."

James' smile faded. "We did," he said. "T-The strange thing is that I did not even realize that until I came to find him. I-I always thought we did not understand one another, but I was wrong. So very wrong. The important thing is that I have found my brother and I intend to take him home."

Essich nodded. "I'm glad," he said. "But the ground is frozen now. 'Twill be difficult to dig him up. Can ye wait until the spring when the ground is softer?"

James looked at Gaira. The idea of spending the next few months in the Highlands, with her, was not a dismal one. In fact, he was rather pleased by it.

"I-I suppose I'll have to," he said. "I'm not leaving without him, so I shall make do until the time comes."

"Do ye have a place tae stay?"

The corner of James' mouth twitched as he and Gaira smiled at one another. "I-It is possible," he said, inferring that she was part of those future plans. "I-I'll find somewhere to stay and something to occupy my time. Meanwhile, I can have a casket built for my brother so we can transport him south. It will give me time to make the necessary preparations."

The man actually seemed a good deal more at peace than he had when he'd first entered the church. He knew where his brother was, he'd been told of his relatively painless passing, and he had recovered items that were precious to him. That was a great relief to Essich, who stepped out from the alcove and motioned to the group.

"Come with me, then," he said. "Some warm drink and bread tae celebrate the life of Johnathan de Lohr before we make the necessary preparations."

Gaira was first, following the reverend, with James and Rafe bringing up the rear. They passed through the cold, candle-lit church and through a door that was near the nave. Exiting into what used to be the cloister centuries ago, James found himself looking up into the clear night sky.

"I-I don't recall ever seeing the stars so bright," he said. "S-Somehow, the world seems a little brighter tonight."

He paused, and Rafe with him, both of them looking up into the sky.

"Feeling better?" Rafe asked.

"A-Aye," James said. Then, he pointed to the sky. "L-Look, there; that star is bigger than the rest."

Rafe could see the one he meant. "*When they saw the star, they rejoiced exceedingly and with great joy,*" he said. When James looked at him, he smiled weakly. "That is from the Bible. It is nearing the time of day of Christ's birth, in fact. It seems to me that you have been given the greatest gift of all this holiday season."

James nodded, thinking on his journey to Calvine, to Inverness. "O-Of everything I thought it would be, it was none of those things," he said. "I-I don't know what I expected, but this journey has been most unexpected in many ways."

Rafe looked over James' shoulder, seeing Gaira as she stood down from them on the walkway with the reverend. "I'm glad she told you what she knew."

James turned to look at Gaira before returning his focus to Rafe. His brow furrowed. "W-What do you mean?" he asked. Then, realization dawned. "Y-You knew about my brother's haversack? You knew she had it?"

Rafe shrugged. "I suspected," he said. "I did not know for certain, but on the night you and I sat together, she was in the chamber. I saw her face as you spoke of your brother and I suspected she knew something. I told her to tell you what she knew and I am glad she did."

That explained it a little better and James turned to look at her again, his gaze lingering on her. "I-I am glad she did, also," he said. "S-She is a thoughtful, warm woman, one I intend to get to know quite well."

Rafe's eyes were glimmering with mirth. "Another gift you have received this holiday season," he said. Then, he looked up at the sky again. "Tell me something, James."

"W-What?"

"Do you believe in miracles?"

James started to speak but stopped himself. Then, he chuckled wryly. "I-I never thought so until I came to the Highlands," he said. "B-But it seems to me that everything that has happened with regards to my brother has been some sort of miracle. I came to know things about my brother that I hadn't known before and I found a woman who knows him, and me, very well. I-I know that sounds odd considering I'd not met Gaira before I came to Calvine, but she's quite… special."

"I know."

"M-My brother left me a letter that was found in his haversack and in the letter, he mentioned praying for a guardian angel for me," James went on. "H-He said that he was my guardian angel on earth and he prayed that God would send me another in his place. I think… I think that Gaira may be that angel. I feel something for her that I cannot describe, but it has something to do with comfort and understanding and…"

"Love?" Rafe interjected.

James grinned, lopsided. "P-Perhaps," he said. "I-I am hopeful."

Rafe smiled faintly, watching James as the man gazed up at the stars again. This wasn't the same young lord he'd met at Balthazar's Inn several days ago. That young lord had been tormented and bitter. The man before him was full of peace.

It was, after all, a season of peace.

Rafe looked back up to the sky and to the bright start in particular.

"Do you know your archangels, James?"

James shook his head. "I-I am afraid I am much like my brother was," he said. "Neither of us were very pious."

The corner of Rafe's lips twitched. "I know that about you," he said. "If you don't know your archangels, then let me explain to you that Raphael is the archangel of healing, both physical and emotional. This is a season when angels walk the earth, a time of miracles. Your brother's prayers were heard, James. Johnathan exchanged one guardian angel for another. And, yes, he is waiting for you in heaven, but not with worms in his eyeballs."

James had been daydreaming as he gazed up at the stars, but Rafe's odd statement caught his attention. "A-Ah, yes," he said. "W-Worms in his eyeballs. I think that was something I wrote to him on more than one occasion when I was younger, but... hold a moment... *how* did you know about that? Did you read that letter, too?"

Rafe grinned, patting him on the shoulder as he turned and headed back towards the church. "That bright star will be gone tonight," he said, pointing upwards. "And so will I."

Confused, James took a few steps after him. "B-But where are you going, Rafe?"

"To find others that need healing. And, James?"

"What?"

"The name is Raphael."

With that, he turned and disappeared into the church. Literally, he disappeared into the darkness. Bewildered, James went after him only to be faced with a vacant church. There was no tall, pale man in white woolen clothing anywhere to be seen. Baffled, James turned towards the door again, processing what he'd been told.

What had happened.

Raphael is the archangel of healing, both physical and emotional. This is a season when angels walk the earth, a time of miracles.

That's what Rafe had said.

The name is Raphael.

Startled, James came to a halt, realizing what he'd just been told. Rushing out into the cloister, he looked into the sky to see that, indeed, the bright star had vanished. Now, it was simply a velvet black sky covered with a sea of diamonds, all of them twinkling brilliantly.

It was an evening full of beauty.

Oddly enough, he didn't doubt Rafe in the least. Now, the man's presence made sense. Everything he had done made sense. The recovery of Johnathan's sword and haversack and letters and the ring made sense. Even Gaira made sense. James hadn't been a man to believe in miracles as he'd said, but tonight, he did.

The pieces of the puzzle had all come together.

On this night of nights, James realized that he had come face to face with his very own guardian angel.

When Gaira asked him later what had become

of Rafe, James simply told her that the man had to leave.

Perhaps there were some miracles better kept to himself.

Part Seven

JAMES AND GAIRA

Year of Our Lord 1747
The month of April

J AMES' FACE WAS buried in Gaira's neck, smelling the sweet musky scent that had the ability to arouse him like nothing else. He could feel her soft breasts against his bare chest, experiencing the sensual movement every time he thrust into her.

Gaira's legs were wrapped around his hips but he unwrapped them, holding them behind the knees, giving him more freedom of movement as he continued to thrust into her sweet and yielding body.

His wife.

Gaira had her hands on his lower back, stroking it, stroking his smooth buttocks as he made love to her. She loved it when he slowed his pace, withdrawing completely only to plunge into her again, slowly. Her hands drifted between their bodies, putting her fingers on his phallus as he joined his body with hers. Nothing seemed to fuel James' desire than her fingers on his manhood.

His climax was instantaneous.

It was the second time that morning he'd taken her, as he'd taken her every single night since the day he'd married her two months earlier. At the Old High Church in Inverness, Reverend Essich had performed the ceremony joining Gaira Dunmore, former heiress to the Earldom of Forth, to James de Lohr, Earl of Worcester. Carrie had been in attendance along with Gaira's mother, who sobbed loudly through the entire thing. When all was said and done, Lord and Lady Worcester signed the parish registrar's book as man and wife.

Much had gone on in the past four months in preparation for returning Johnathan de Lohr to Lioncross Abbey, home of generations of de Lohrs. James had rented a little cottage in Inverness, right on the River Ness, a place for him and his wife to stay while he made the necessary arrangements.

Gaira's mother, Helen, chose to return to Calvine after their marriage, to the home she had shared with her husband for many years, leaving her daughter to start her new life as the Countess of Worcester. Gaira and James quickly integrated into the Inverness community, with Gaira becoming popular with the locals. She was bright, educated, and entertained an excellent crowd, and the women of the village tittered over her handsome husband.

Truth be told, so did Gaira.

It was the life she never thought she would have.

But, God, did she love it.

This morning, however, would prove to be their last morning in Inverness, as preparations for digging up Johnathan's grave were coming to a head. In months past, a beautiful coffin had been built of Scots pine, heavy and well-made as befitting the former Earl of Worcester. The man who made it was also the wheelwright in the village, and his skill had been beyond compare. He'd carved beautiful lines into the coffin and, at the strange request of the current Earl of Worcester, managed to carve some worms up near the head of the coffin.

He was being well paid, so he didn't ask questions.

But to James, those worms meant everything.

Now, the lined coffin was waiting for its occupant and arrangements had been made to begin the digging at sunrise. Spring had come early this year and the ground was already softened enough to dig. As James lay next to his naked wife, his arms wrapped around her, he could see that it was about sunrise now. Face in the side of her head, he groaned softly.

"T-They will be waiting for me," he mumbled. "I-I cannot keep my brother waiting."

Gaira yawned. "Do ye want me tae go with ye?"

James opened his eyes, thinking on what this day would bring. "I-I would like you to," he said softly. "T-This is why we came to Inverness in the first place. Let us greet Johnathan together. I can tell him of our marriage."

It was a very big day in their lives, one that Gaira knew her husband was both looking forward to and dreading. She smiled, trying to lighten the mood.

"Would he approve of ye marrying a serving wench, then?"

James chuckled. "S-She's not a serving wench," he said, lightly slapping her bare buttocks. "S-She's a countess. A veritable goddess. Aye, he would approve."

Gaira laughed softly, wrapping her arms

around him and hugging him tightly. She kissed him gently with her soft lips, feeling him grow amorous in an instant, ready to take her again. But there wasn't time and she pushed him away.

"Get up, my bonny lad," she said, sitting up with the coverlet held to her naked breasts. "Today is a big day and ye mustna be late."

With a heavy sigh, James sat up beside her. There was something in his manner that suggested he was becoming moody towards what he was about to face and Gaira looked at him with sympathy.

"It will be all right," she said softly. "Dunna fret over what ye must do. It has tae be done."

He nodded faintly. "I-I know," he said, sounding resigned. "T-This is the day I have waited for, yet there is something about it that is inherently sad. I am going to see my brother today."

"I know."

"I-It will be his body, in whatever state it is in."

"And ye dunna feel ready for it?"

He shrugged. "G-God knows, I should be," he said. "S-Since it has been so cold, he should be well preserved and I have been prepared for this moment ever since we were told of his death, but still… seeing him will make all of this a reality. My brother is truly dead."

Gaira smiled sadly at him putting a gentle

hand on his cheek. "He is," she said with quiet finality. "But he met his death well. Ye know he did. It's time tae bring him home."

James held her hand against his face, turning to kiss the palm. "A-And I shall," he said. But then, he grew quiet. "I-I have been thinking of something else."

"What of?"

"F-From his last letter to me," he said. "J-Johnny asked that I leave something of him behind to watch over the brave men who would never make it home. He wanted to ensure they were protected. I have been thinking long and hard about that request."

"And?"

He lifted his left hand, the one with the de Lohr signet ring on it. He gazed at the heirloom for a long, intense moment.

"C-Carrie told me that when she went through the things that were brought to her, she removed any valuables away for safe keeping," he said. "Y-You said the same thing."

Gaira leaned against him, looking at the ring as well. "In her Chamber of Sorrows," she said. "She has hole in the floor where she keeps a box of the valuable things she has found."

"W-What is in there?"

Gaira reflected on the small, square wooden box shoved into its little niche in the floor.

"Gold," she said. "Gold coinage and other valuables. It seems strange that men would carry such precious things to a battlefield, but they did. There are gems in the box, rings and the like. Why do ye ask?"

James held up the ring, inspecting it in the weak light.

"B-Because I am going to leave this in the box, too."

Gaira's eyes widened when she realized what he meant. "The signet ring?" she gasped. "But... *why*? Ye came all the way tae Scotland for the thing. It belongs tae ye. Why would ye leave it behind?"

James was studying the ruby eyes, the golden lion face. "I-I am not sure I can explain, but I will try," he said. "J-Johnny was wearing this when he died trying to save men. Everything inside me tells me that I have no right to take it away from this place. He asked me to leave something of him behind to watch over the brave dead, and it seems to me that this ring is the most logical thing to leave behind. The power of the de Lohr crest can watch over those men who fought, and died, by Johnny's command. Does that make sense? I feel as if, by all rights, the ring should remain here with those who died for it. For Johnny. I have no right to take it away from them."

There was that tender soul again, the one

Gaira loved so well. Perhaps she didn't exactly understand it all but, then again, men in battle shared a special bond. Brothers shared a special bond. Clearly, this meant a great deal to James and she knew he hadn't made the decision lightly.

Leaning over, she kissed him on the cheek.

"If that's what ye want tae do, then do it," she said. "At least ye'll know where it is, for always. It willna be lost, but simply standing watch over the dead of Culloden in Carrie's chamber."

"E-Exactly," he said, looking at her. "I-I knew you would understand. One of the many things I love about you. And who knows? Maybe one day, a de Lohr will wear the ring again. But for now, it belongs to Johnny and that room full of ghosts. That is where it shall stay."

"And ye feel confident with that decision?"

"I-I do. More than anything."

Gaira kissed him again and, for a moment, they smiled at one another, feeling the warmth and love between them that was stronger than anything on earth.

Stronger than death.

Stronger than a ring.

In the days to come, the de Lohr signet ring found a home in a dingy little box buried in the floor of Carrie's Chamber of Sorrows. Exactly thirty-one days later, Johnathan de Lohr was laid to rest in Lioncross Abbey's great chapel, taking his rightful place among his ancestors as his brother, his brother's wife, his mother, and several de Lohr relatives witnessed the interment.

But not before a letter from James was packed against Johnathan's stilled heart before they closed the lid forever.

A letter from one brother to another.

My Dearest Johnny –

And so, our letter writing campaign comes to an end.

From your petulant, ridiculous younger brother, you have my deepest thanks for the path my life has taken. It seems odd to say such a thing, but in your death, I found my life and my purpose. I pray that I can live up to your example, for it is one I shall always worship.

What I should have told you in life, I will tell you in death. If you do not wait for me in heaven, I shall be very angry, for it will be my greatest honor to tell you how much I love you the moment I see you again. How much I have always loved you, my brother. I am sorry I wished worms in your eyeballs. I did not mean it.

Much.

Until we meet again,
James

෪ THE END ෨

Want to read Johnathan de Lohr's story?
Read *The Earl of Christmas Past* by Kerrigan
Byrne.

Kathryn Le Veque Novels

Medieval Romance:

De Wolfe Pack Series:
Warwolfe
The Wolfe
Nighthawk
ShadowWolfe
DarkWolfe
A Joyous de Wolfe Christmas
BlackWolfe
Serpent
A Wolfe Among Dragons
Scorpion
StormWolfe
Dark Destroyer
The Lion of the North
Walls of Babylon
The Best Is Yet To Be

De Wolfe Pack Generations:
WolfeHeart
WolfeStrike
WolfeSword

The de Russe Legacy:
The Falls of Erith
Lord of War: Black Angel
The Iron Knight
Beast
The Dark One: Dark Knight
The White Lord of Wellesbourne
Dark Moon

Dark Steel
A de Russe Christmas Miracle
Dark Warrior

The de Lohr Dynasty:
While Angels Slept
Rise of the Defender
Steelheart
Shadowmoor
Silversword
Spectre of the Sword
Unending Love
Archangel
A Blessed de Lohr Christmas

The Brothers de Lohr:
The Earl in Winter

Lords of East Anglia:
While Angels Slept
Godspeed

Great Lords of le Bec:
Great Protector

House of de Royans:
Lord of Winter
To the Lady Born
The Centurion

Lords of Eire:
Echoes of Ancient Dreams
Blacksword
The Darkland

Ancient Kings of Anglecynn:
The Whispering Night
Netherworld

Battle Lords of de Velt:
The Dark Lord
Devil's Dominion
Bay of Fear
The Dark Lord's First Christmas

Reign of the House of de Winter:
Lespada
Swords and Shields

De Reyne Domination:
Guardian of Darkness
With Dreams
The Fallen One

House of d'Vant:
Tender is the Knight (House of d'Vant)
The Red Fury (House of d'Vant)

The Dragonblade Series:
Fragments of Grace
Dragonblade
Island of Glass
The Savage Curtain
The Fallen One

Great Marcher Lords of de Lara
Dragonblade

House of St. Hever
Fragments of Grace
Island of Glass
Queen of Lost Stars

Lords of Pembury:
The Savage Curtain

Lords of Thunder: The de Shera Brotherhood Trilogy
The Thunder Lord

The Thunder Warrior
The Thunder Knight

The Great Knights of de Moray:
Shield of Kronos
The Gorgon

The House of De Nerra:
The Promise
The Falls of Erith
Vestiges of Valor
Realm of Angels

Highland Warriors of Munro:
The Red Lion
Deep Into Darkness

The House of de Garr:
Lord of Light
Realm of Angels

Saxon Lords of Hage:
The Crusader
Kingdom Come

High Warriors of Rohan:
High Warrior

The House of Ashbourne:
Upon a Midnight Dream

The House of D'Aurilliac:
Valiant Chaos

The House of De Dere:
Of Love and Legend

St. John and de Gare Clans:
The Warrior Poet

The House of de Bretagne:
The Questing

The House of Summerlin:
The Legend

The Kingdom of Hendocia:
Kingdom by the Sea

The Executioner Knights:
By the Unholy Hand
The Mountain Dark
Starless
The Promise (also Noble Knights of de Nerra)
A Time of End
Winter of Solace
Lord of the Shadows
Lord of the Sky

Contemporary Romance:

Kathlyn Trent/Marcus Burton Series:
Valley of the Shadow
The Eden Factor
Canyon of the Sphinx

The American Heroes Anthology Series:
The Lucius Robe
Fires of Autumn
Evenshade
Sea of Dreams
Purgatory

Other non-connected Contemporary Romance:
Lady of Heaven
Darkling, I Listen
In the Dreaming Hour
River's End
The Fountain

Sons of Poseidon:
The Immortal Sea

Pirates of Britannia Series (with Eliza Knight):
Savage of the Sea by Eliza Knight
Leader of Titans by Kathryn Le Veque
The Sea Devil by Eliza Knight
Sea Wolfe by Kathryn Le Veque

Note: All Kathryn's novels are designed to be read as stand-alones, although many have cross-over characters or cross-over family groups. Novels that are grouped together have related characters or family groups. You will notice that some series have the same books; that is because they are cross-overs. A hero in one book may be the secondary character in another.

There is NO reading order except by chronology, but even in that case, you can still read the books as stand-alones. No novel is connected to another by a cliff hanger, and every book has an HEA.

Series are clearly marked. All series contain the same characters or family groups except the American Heroes Series, which is an anthology with unrelated characters.

For more information, find it in **A Reader's Guide to the Medieval World of Le Veque**.

About Kathryn Le Veque

KATHRYN LE VEQUE is a USA TODAY Bestselling author, an Amazon All-Star author, and a #1 bestselling, award-winning, multi-published author in Medieval Historical Romance and Historical Fiction. She has been featured in the NEW YORK TIMES and on USA TODAY's HEA blog.

Kathryn's Medieval Romance novels have been called "detailed", "highly romantic", and "character-rich". She crafts great adventures of love, battles, passion, and romance in the High Middle Ages. More than that, she writes for both women AND men – an unusual crossover for a romance author – and Kathryn has many male readers who enjoy her stories because of the male perspective, the action, the passion, and the adventure.

Kathryn loves to hear from her readers. Please find Kathryn on Facebook at Kathryn Le Veque, Author, or join her on Twitter @kathrynleveque, and don't forget to visit her website and sign up for her blog at www.kathrynleveque.com.

Please follow Kathryn on Bookbub for the latest releases and sales.